6/03

Ali and the Magic Stew

by *Shulamith Levey Oppenheim*

Illustrated by Winslow Pels

Boyds Mills Press

Published by Boyds Mills Press, Inc.
A Highlights Company
815 Church Street
Honesdale, Pennsylvania 18431
Printed in China
Visit our website at www.boydsmillspress.com

U.S. Cataloging-in-Publication Data
(Library of Congress Standards)

Oppenheim, Shulamith Levey.
Ali and the magic stew / by Shulamith Levey Oppenheim ; illustrated by
Winslow Pels.— 1st ed.
[32] p. : col. ill. ; cm.
Summary: Guided by a beggar he so often shunned, a young, spoiled boy in Persia
must quickly collect ingredients for a healing stew to make for his dying father.
ISBN: 1-56397-869-5
1. Iran — Juvenile fiction. 2. Humility — Fiction — Juvenile literature.
[1. Iran — Fiction. 2. Humility — Fiction .] I. Pels, Winslow. II. Title.
[E] 21 2002 AC CIP
2001090182

First edition, 2002
The text of this book is set in 15-point Tiepolo Book.

10 9 8 7 6 5 4 3 2 1

For my daughter, Claire, and my daughters-in-law, Martha and Layne,
who bring magic into my life with their love (and their cooking, of course!)
—S. L. O.

For the gentlehearted family of Taruni and Yadu, and in memory of Qisma'at
—W. P.

L

ong ago, in a land called Persia, there lived a boy named Ali ibn Ali. His father was a wealthy merchant. His mother was a woman of great beauty and even greater kindness. His home was a palace where fountains overflowed into deep reflecting pools. As he had no brothers or sisters, he was, so everyone said, the apricot of his parents' eye.

But fortunate as Ali ibn Ali was in worldly gifts, he was most unfortunate in that he had grown spoiled and selfish.

"I don't like these grapes!" A handful of fruit went flying through the air. Ali was sitting cross-legged with a small black monkey on his shoulder. "Neither does Layla! They are fit only for the beggar who fouls our gate!"

At that moment Ali's parents entered the room. Now, if Ali had one spot in his heart that raced with love, it was for his parents.

"What are we hearing?" His father waved his hands at his son. "That is no way to speak, beloved child."

His mother kissed Ali on both cheeks. They sat down beside him.

"These grapes are rotten, Father." Ali threw his arms around his father's neck. "They are fit only for the bowl of that filthy beggar who crowds our gate."

Ali wrinkled up his nose and stroked his father's cheek. "Why do you allow him to sit there?"

His mother took Ali's slim, ringed fingers in hers. "A true Muslim gives to the poor, the crippled, the homeless, the hungry. That beggar is all of these." Layla jumped off Ali's shoulder and onto the lap of Ali's mother.

"And," his father put his palms together before his face, "as he chooses to bless our gate and accept our food, there he shall remain. Now I have something to tell you."

Ali jumped up, his face suddenly flushed. He saw his father was dressed for traveling. "Father, are you going away? Mother, tell him he mustn't go away again. Not so soon. We're very lonely when he's gone. So is Layla." His mother said nothing, but Ali knew she, too, wished her husband to stay.

"It will be but for a few days, my beloved ones. Ali, take care of your mother. And no more ugly tempers. Such behavior is not acceptable at any age!"

That evening Ali and his mother stood in the palace courtyard as the merchant galloped off on his favorite white horse, followed by three servants, their saddlebags bulging with spices and gems. But in two days he was brought back on a litter, racked with fever and pain in all his limbs.

During the next days a steady parade of doctors and wise men examined the suffering merchant. Each left mixes of herbs and potions, but emerged utterly bewildered.

Ali held Layla close under his arm. Whenever his eyes overflowed with tears, the monkey gently wiped the boy's cheeks with her small paws.

"What shall we do, Layla? Mother sits by Father's bed day and night cooling his face with rose water. *We must help*."

Ali tiptoed to the door of his father's room and knocked softly. "Come," his mother answered. His father lay in a high, canopied bed. Ali had never seen his mother's face so pale and sad.

"The fever is raging, my Ali," she whispered. "He does not eat or drink, and his words . . ." She put a hand to her mouth, stifling a sob. "He mutters, but I cannot understand him."

Ali leaned close to his father's face. "Father, it's Ali. Do you wish to tell us something?" The invalid made a move to lift his hand, but it fell back limply onto the coverlet.

"Shhhhh . . . llla," his voice was barely audible. "Mmmmm ba, kah . . . kah . . . la."

Ali turned toward his mother. His eyes were bright. "I think, Mother, though I don't know why, but I think Father is trying to say *shula kalambar*. Would he ask for shula kalambar, Mother? It's a tasty stew, but . . ."

"Shula kalambar? It certainly isn't a favorite of his." His mother was as confused as her son. "It *is* tasty, but there are so many other delicacies that he enjoys far more—honey cakes and rice creams and grilled lamb with mint and allspice."

Ali knelt down beside the bed. "Am I right, Father? You're saying shula kalambar?" There was a slight but distinct movement of his father's head.

Without another word Ali raced from the room and across the courtyard to the kitchens.

"Cook, we must have shula kalambar," he commanded in his imperious tone. "This instant! My father requests it!"

"I regret, young master," the cook bowed, "we have lentils and garlic but no spinach or coriander. These two must be the freshest possible."

Ali stamped his foot. "Then get them!"

Head still bowed, the cook answered, "My kitchen boys are not here, young master, and I cannot leave. There is baklava in the oven for my mistress, your honored mother. I—"

"I don't care about you!" Ali shook his head in rage. Then, "Very well, I shall get the ingredients myself!"

He ran to his chamber, where he took coins from a bronze box and tucked them into the pocket of his silk trousers. Again he raced across the courtyard to the outer gate. As he passed through, he tripped and fell over the beggar's bowl. "Pig!" Ali could feel the blood oozing from his knee. With a sharp intake of breath, he pulled up against the gate, brushing the beggar's shoulder.

"Steady, Ali ibn Ali." The beggar's voice was musical, young. Ali did not recall it having such a lilt. "There is time before the stalls close."

The words stunned Ali. "How did you know I was going to the market stalls?" His voice held the usual disdain.

The unfortunate shifted position. "I know," he answered slowly. "I also know you are correct. Your father *did* ask for shula kalambar. And I know that shula kalambar has great healing powers.

"But," he raised a long, knobbed finger, "for the stew to work, *all* the ingredients must be purchased with coins begged from the street. *All* ingredients. Garlic, coriander, lentils, spinach."

"Begged from the street!" Anger and irritation shot through Ali's slight frame. "Then give me what you have in your bowl. I will give you gold coins in exchange."

"Ah, Ali ibn Ali, it is not that simple. These coins must be gained by a family member for the healing properties to work."

family member! Ali looked down at the beggar. "Why should I believe *you*? You sit here in the dust by my father's gate and by his grace. What do you know of the world?"

The beggar looked up at the boy, his heavy-lidded eyes half-closed. "There is no reason to believe me, young master. But if you wish to save your father, heed my words."

Layla was racing round and round Ali's feet, chittering and chattering and pulling at his trousers. Ali's head whirled. Strangely, very strangely, every bone in his body was suddenly pushing him to do as the beggar instructed.

However much he abhorred this creature, he must do what was necessary so that his father would be well and the roses would again bloom in his mother's cheeks.

"Then *I* shall beg," he replied. With that, Ali ibn Ali threw back his shoulders and straightened his turban with its diamond plume. "No one will deny me. I have only to ask."

As Ali turned to leave, the beggar caught him by the belt of his tunic. The boy recoiled, but the beggar held fast. "Begged from the street, in the clothes of a beggar, hunched as a beggar, with a beggar's bowl." The man smiled up at him.

By now Ali's head was throbbing. Fine blue veins rose up under the skin of his temples. He knew precious time was wasting. Quickly he removed his turban and tunic. As he did, the beggar threw off his ragged cloak with an agility that belied his wizened appearance and handed it up to the boy. In return, Ali laid the turban and the tunic next to the beggar. Then he smeared his face with dust, threw the cloak over his head, put Layla back on his shoulder, and set out.

Bent, and with an ache in his heart, Ali held the bowl at arm's length, averting his eyes from the scornful gaze of passersby. "Please, sir," Ali ran toward a richly dressed man and woman, "please, lady, for my father who is dying. For a stew to heal him. Please, for the love of Allah."

The couple sneered, but the woman opened her gold mesh purse and dropped a coin into the bowl. As Ali leaned forward, the man shoved him aside with a force that sent the boy and the monkey skidding across the cobbles. The coin flew from the bowl.

"A dying father! Now there's a new one. What lies these pigs invent to take our gold!"

Ali crawled after the coin, heedless of the jeers. "Out of sight, filth and son of filth," the man called after him.

It was Layla who retrieved the coin and the bowl. Ali stood up, and the tears that had been brimming in his eyes ran down his cheeks, leaving streaks in the dirt and grime. He felt a soft paw touch each eye. "It's all right, Layla. We must beg enough to buy the lentils and garlic and coriander and spinach. We *must*. But how can people be so cruel? I've feelings, too, under these rags."

So Ali ibn Ali drew the cloak tightly about him and started out again, repeating his pleas, until the sun was low behind the mountains and his limbs could barely crouch. Jeers of "Fool" and "Filth" and "Useless piece of flesh" and scenes of disgust and shame were repeated again and again. Finally, as darkness fell, there were enough coins in the bowl. Ali raced to the market. He found one tiny stand still open. His hands trembled as he paid for his purchases. Layla clung to Ali's arm, her tail wound loosely around his neck. With the precious items wrapped in a sleeve of the cloak, Ali raced back to the palace.

The beggar was sitting as Ali had left him, his chin on his chest. The tunic and turban lay beside him. Ali stopped a moment to catch his breath. "I pray to Allah you are right, old man," the boy whispered. "It's terrible how unkind people can be, because they thought I was poor, because I was begging, because . . ."

He stopped. Something tugged in his chest.

The beggar opened one eye. "Now that you have begged and have obtained the ingredients for the stew, you had better have the shula kalambar prepared immediately, Ali ibn Ali."

Ali fairly galloped to the kitchen. The chief cook was about to toss him out until he revealed himself. Ali requested *politely*, to his own stupefaction as well as to everyone else's, that the stew be prepared instantly.

With Layla on his back, Ali carried the steaming shula kalambar past the lion fountain to his father's room.

He put a finger to his lips in response to his mother's amazement at the sight of him in rags, his face a smudge of dust and grime. "I'll tell you everything later, beloved mother. Now Father must eat."

Ali's mother drew her chair closer to the bed and put her hand under her husband's head. Ali sat down beside his father.

"Eat, my beloved husband, eat," she urged, as Ali put a spoonful to his father's lips.

"Eat, Father, for Mother, for me, for Layla, for yourself above all." To himself he added, "Please, Allah, let this stew heal my father. Let the beggar be right. I will give him anything he desires if my father is cured. I have learned so much these last hours. I—"

"Ali!" His mother gave a cry. "Look at your father's face. The ashes have gone from his skin. Is there not a rosy hue blushing his cheeks?"

It was true. The invalid was breathing more lightly. His eyelids fluttered, then a smile began to play about his lips. A moment later his eyes opened. Ali could barely hold the next spoonful steady, so great was his joy.

"Give me the bowl, beloved." And Ali's mother took the stew from her son. "I will feed him the rest. You must wash from head to toe and throw away that ragged cloak you're wearing. How in Allah's name . . . ?"

"No, Ali, my son." It was his father speaking, in a clear, strong voice. "Do not throw away the cloak. Let it ever be a reminder to you that the gentle heart brings life and joy."

"I will *never* forget, Father. And thank you." Ali kissed his father's hand, and, leaving the room, he ran back to the gate of the palace. Seeing the beggar, he fell on his knees and, in a gentle voice, asked, "May I keep your cloak? My father will provide you with a new one. Maybe two. As many as you'd like."

The beggar took up a stick that lay beside him and, with great effort, started to pull himself up. "Keep the cloak, Ali ibn Ali. Keep it as a reminder of the pain unkindness brings. Don't forget to take your own clothes back. And tell your honorable father I accept his gift."

Ali put his arms around the beggar's shoulders to steady him. "Where are you going? I want you to stay."

"I am going and I am staying," the beggar nodded gravely. Then his face burst into a mass of smiling creases. "I am staying and I am going. Your father will grow strong. Roses will again bloom in your mother's cheeks.

"And you,"—the beggar touched Ali's forehead—"will be a source of pride and joy to your parents now and in their old age." And with that, the beggar melted into the darkness.